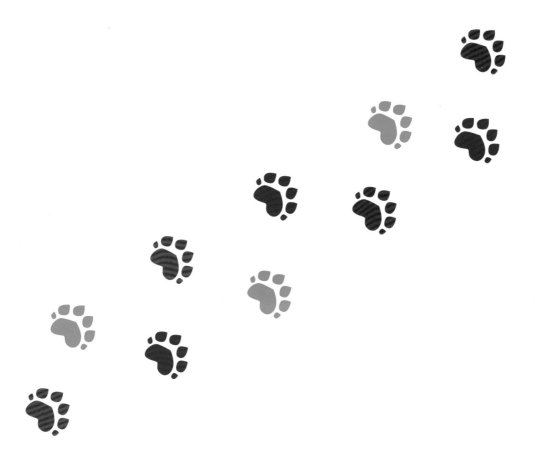

ISBN- 978-0-9860214-0-4 (Hardcover)
LCCN- 2012914300
1283 Murner Rd. Gaylord MI, 49735
http://www.facebook.com/TheAdventuresOfLilyAndAva

# Dedication Page

The book series The Adventures of Lily and Ava is dedicated to my two daughters Lily and Ryan who are the inspiration behind me writing children's books. I would like to thank all of those who have had a hand in helping me develop my book series, and a special thanks to Crystal Bowan (Editor) and Jim Dombrowski (Illustrator).

To: _____

From: _____

*Gordon Briley* (signature)

THE ADVENTURES OF
*Lily & Ava*

# New Friendships

❀ ❀ ❀ ❀

Written by Gordon Briley

Illustrated by Jim Dombrowski

Hi! This is my friend Ava, and I am Lily.

We like to goof around and we're always being silly.

These are the stories about things we have done.

Come along with us, and have some fun.

Our adventures began on the day that we met.

It was an amazing day that we'll never forget.

Ava's parents were moving to the house next door;

I've never seen a house that scary before.


The house was creepy and really old,

It may be haunted, or so I've been told.

They could still turn around; it's not too late.

Probably won't make it past the gate.

I watched as their truck pulled in slow,

now it's too late—here they go.

I ran from the window I didn't want to see,

this was all too much for me.


I went into my room and decided to play.

My parents came in and began to say,

"We're going next door to go say hi."

I said, "No way! How about good-bye!"

My parents made me go and led me outside.

That house is scary; I just wanted to hide.

They pushed me up the stairs to the old scary house.

I walked very slowly—quiet like a mouse.


My mom reached out to ring the bell.

This wasn't good— I could just tell.

"Let's just go!" I yelled as I turned to go back.

Then I heard a little voice say, "Hey, come back!"

I slowly peeked from behind my dad,

and what I saw wasn't bad.

There stood a girl holding a little kitten.

I could see a tag where a name was written.


Tink was the name that I could see,

she looked really nice, cute as can be.

"My name is Ava and my kitten has six toes."

It jumped from her hands and there she goes.

"My name is Lily, I'll help you catch your cat."

"Sure Lily, I would love help with that!

She moves really fast; so we have to be quick.

Can't make a sound, not a lick."


"I'll go left; and you can go right.

Don't let her out of your sight."

The kitten ran in the yard and up a tree.

"Oh no, Ava! That's too high for me."

"Maybe we could use a rope or ladder."

But Tink was scared and getting sadder.

Ava yelled, "Look in your yard at that bouncy thing."

"Yes of course—my mini trampoline!"


We ran and grabbed it and pulled it under the tree.

"Come here, Kitty, come jump to me."

Tink just sat there and let out a cry.

"It's okay, Kitty, just give it a try."

"Ava, look! She's moving—she's going to go.

That's right, Kitty, nice and slow."

I bounced on the trampoline to show her how,

"Come here, Tink, do it now."


The kitten jumped and bounced so high,

and over my head she did fly.

Tink was spinning around like a fan,

then she landed in a garbage can.

The can tipped over and she was stuck inside;

she rolled down the driveway for a dizzy ride.

When the can finally came to a stop,

the kitten flew right out the top.



Tink landed in the back of their truck.

"We've got her now! She's run out of luck!"

We saw a box shaking that was labeled CRAFTING.

We looked inside and started laughing.

CRAFTING

"Oh no, Ava! What did she do?"

Tink was colored green, red, and blue.

She was covered in paint from her tail to nose.

She jumped out of the box, and there she goes!


"Can't stop now—this is way too fun!"

"Let's go get her, she's back on the run."

Tink then ran to the edge of the street.

A van was sitting there and she jumped in the seat.

The man who was driving yelled, "Hey come see this cat!

I've never seen anything look like that."

A man appeared with a camera pointed at us,

"What's going on, what's all the fuss?"


He looked at the cat and began to smile.

"Haven't seen anything like this in a while!

Here's your kitten now hold it tight.

You're going to be on the news tonight."

We couldn't believe what we were hearing.

We jumped up and down and started cheering.

"Lily, what a day, I am so glad that we met!"

"Ava, have you noticed that Tink's still wet?"


The paint had smeared on her shirt and left a design.

"Let me see her, Ava, I want one on mine."

She handed me Tink and I held her against my chest.

This was awesome! We're the best!

Today I learned that I shouldn't be so afraid,

you never know when there's a friend to be made.

From this day on we were the best of friends,

and this is how our first adventure ends.

Want to see the real Lily and Ava?
Go to http://www.facebook.com/TheAdventuresOfLilyAndAva

I hope you enjoyed the adventure!

Watch for Vol. 2, "A Day at Play," coming early 2013!

Please visit the Facebook fan page and share your comments,
questions, and even share your ideas for future adventures.